I0619013

Because I Can

By: Allison McWood

Annelid Press

This book is a work of fiction. The characters, incidents and dialogue are drawn from the author's imagination and are not to be construed as real. Any resemblance to actual events or persons, living or dead, is entirely coincidental.

Because I Can
Copyright © 2020 by Allison McWood.
All rights reserved. No part of this book may be used or reproduced in any manner whatsoever without written permission except in the case of brief quotations embodied in critical articles and reviews. For information address Annelid Press.
www.annelidpress.com.
FIRST EDITION

Cover photo featuring: Sandy Jobin-Bevans

ISBN: 978-1-7772203-1-0

Cast List

Dr. Mendax ....a sociopathic doctor

SHYLIE...a young woman

FLOYD ....an insecure male nurse

BOGDAN..a Romanian janitor

SCENE ONE

A hospital. There is a split stage. On one side of the wall, there is an examination room, where SHYLIE is sitting nervously on an examination table and DR. MENDAX is writing something in a chart. On the other side of the wall is the hallway of the hospital. There is a door in the hallway, there is o the janitor's broom closet. The door remains closed. In the hallway is BOGDAN, perpetually mopping, even as the scenes in the examination room occur. As he mops, he occasionally overhears the goings-on in the examination room. Disapproving, he will shake his head in disbelief and disgust as the ludicrous things in the examination room ensue. Even so, BOGDAN seems to be minding his own business, always mopping, always present. BOGDAN speaks in a Romanian accent.

MENDAX   Remove your shirt.

SHYLIE   What?

MENDAX   Take it off.

SHYLIE   But...

MENDAX   Strip.

SHYLIE   Dr. Mendax...

MENDAX   Everything comes off. Bra. Panties. The whole bit.

SHYLIE   But you're a podiatrist.

MENDAX   Are you questioning my judgment?

SHYLIE   But my foot...

MENDAX   I know what I'm doing.

SHYLIE   No!

MENDAX   I have a medical degree.

SHYLIE   I'm...I'm a little embarrassed.

MENDAX   Why are you here?

SHYLIE   Because my foot...

MENDAX   No. I mean, why have you come to me specifically?

SHYLIE   My doctor referred me to a podiatrist because I have a
            problem with my foot.

MENDAX   No. You came to me because you trust me with your
            life.

SHYLIE   Life?

MENDAX   Health.

SHYLIE   Health?

MENDAX   Feet, then. The point is, I am an expert in my field and I know more than you do about complicated, medical thingies.

SHYLIE   Maybe I should...

MENDAX   What? Maybe you should what? Go to another podiatrist?

SHYLIE   I don't know.

MENDAX   I challenge you to find another doctor. No podiatrist in town is taking new patients and those who are have a waiting list of up to three years.

SHYLIE   Why are you being so mean?

MENDAX   Mean? Shylie, are you aware of the suicide rate among doctors? The stress of my job is crippling and your reluctance to co-operate is not improving matters. Would you look at that? My pulse is racing like a greyhound.

SHYLIE   That's no reason to be mean.

MENDAX   The word is gruff. And how can you blame me for being frustrated? I know more than you and here you are speaking to me as though my cerebrum is on sabbatical.

SHYLIE   What?

MENDAX   I am not an idiot.

SHYLIE   I never said...

Enter FLOYD with a corpse.

FLOYD   Where should I put this one?

MENDAX   In the pile with the others.

FLOYD   Done.

FLOYD crosses the stage and exits.

SHYLIE   I never said you were an idiot.

FLOYD crosses stage in the opposite direction, without the corpse and exits.

SHYLIE   I am quite self-conscious about my feet.

MENDAX   Is there something wrong with them?

SHYLIE   Not really. I mean, the left one hurts, but...

MENDAX   Then what is the problem?

SHYLIE   Feet embarrass me.

Enter FLOYD with another corpse.

FLOYD   Here's another.

MENDAX   The pile, Susan.

FLOYD   My name is Floyd.

                              FLOYD crosses stage and exits with the corpse

MENDAX   Why aren't you naked?

SHYLIE   Aren't I entitled to an...

MENDAX   Explanation. Everyone wants an explanation.

SHYLIE   It's only a foot examination.

                              FLOYD crosses the stage in the opposite direction, without the corpse, and exits through the door of the examination room.

MENDAX   Remove your socks then.

SHYLIE   My socks?

MENDAX   Good God, woman. Is that so unreasonable?

                              Enter FLOYD with another corpse.

FLOYD   The pile?

MENDAX   Yes, Susan.

FLOYD	Floyd.
SHYLIE	What pile?
MENDAX	Attend to Shylie while I get the results from her X-rays.
FLOYD	Yes, Dr. Mendax.

Exit MENDAX.

SHYLIE	Dr. Floyd...Dr. Floyd?
FLOYD	Hmmm? Oh, I'm not a...That is, I'm not exactly a...
SHYLIE	You're not a doctor?
FLOYD	I'm sort of a...I guess you could say...I'm likened unto a...
SHYLIE	Resident?
FLOYD	No.
SHYLIE	Intern?
FLOYD	Nurse.
SHYLIE	Nurse?
FLOYD	I have a very important job.
SHYLIE	Floyd...

FLOYD   I do lots of disgusting jobs that would make most women squeamish.

SHYLIE   Floyd...

FLOYD   Bed pans.

SHYLIE   Floyd...

FLOYD   Soiled bandages.

SHYLIE   Floyd...

FLOYD   Needles...

SHYLIE   Floyd...

FLOYD   Really big needles.

SHYLIE   Who are those people?

FLOYD   People?

SHYLIE   In the pile?

FLOYD   Those aren't people. They're corpses.

SHYLIE   A pile of corpses?

FLOYD   Former patients of Dr. Mendax.

SHYLIE   *(attempting to leave)* Excuse me.

FLOYD	*(stopping her)* Don't be worried. You are in excellent hands.
SHYLIE	But...
FLOYD	Dr. Mendax knows what he's doing.
SHYLIE	But...
FLOYD	Dr. Mendax gave each of those corpses six months to live and every one of them died six months to the day.
SHYLIE	You don't say.
FLOYD	Dr. Mendax has quite a skill.
SHYLIE	They died?
FLOYD	Six months to the day.
SHYLIE	But Dr. Mendax is a podiatrist.
FLOYD	That's the genius of it. Who would have thought a person could die from an ingrown toenail or a corn?
SHYLIE	Dead? All of them?
FLOYD	That's what I hear. You see, I'm new.
SHYLIE	New.
FLOYD	Been here three weeks. But Dr. Mendax filled me in on stuff.

SHYLIE   Really.

FLOYD   I don't know what I'd do without Dr. Mendax. He made my transition painless.

SHYLIE   Painless.

FLOYD   He's so sage. You get used to the mood swings.

Enter MENDAX.

MENDAX   Fops. All of them.

FLOYD   What's going on?

MENDAX   Shylie's X-rays are missing.

FLOYD   Typical.

MENDAX   That lab is run by monkeys.

FLOYD   Not everyone can be as smart as you.

MENDAX   You would think that someone in this enormous building would know what was going on. I mean, the tests were run only hours ago.

FLOYD   Things around here seem to always slip through the cracks.

MENDAX   Bureaucratic nightmare.

SHYLIE   I'm feeling much better. Maybe I'll just...

MENDAX   Sit. I haven't yet told you how you feel.

SHYLIE   Really, I...*(gets up and cringes when she puts pressure on her foot)*

FLOYD   You're cringing.

MENDAX   Very good, Susan. We should get you a job in diagnostics.

FLOYD   My name is...

> *MENDAX abruptly grabs SHYLIE'S bare foot and investigates it.*

MENDAX   Hmmm...My...My, my, my, my...Exactly what I suspected. Susan, come here and look at this.

> *FLOYD examines SHYLIE'S foot.*

FLOYD   A plantar wart.

MENDAX   Repugnant, but true. Susan, get the saw.

FLOYD   The what?

MENDAX   You *do* understand what a plantar wart *is?*

FLOYD   I thought some ointment...

MENDAX   Do you have a medical degree?

FLOYD   No.

MENDAX   Get the…

FLOYD   Ointment?

MENDAX   That's what I said.

FLOYD   I'll get the ointment.

                              Exit FLOYD.

MENDAX   *(to SHYLIE)* Inferiors. I'll flog her later.

SHYLIE   Dr. Mendax?

MENDAX   You'd best get your affairs in order.

SHYLIE   Affairs?

MENDAX   You have six months.

SHYLIE   To live?

MENDAX   I'm never wrong.

SCENE TWO

> *BOGDAN is mopping in the hallway. The door to the janitor's broom closet remains closed as BOGDAN mops. From behind the door, there is banging, as though someone wants out of the closet. BOGDAN notices the banging, but once it stops, he continues mopping. The banging continues and BOGDAN becomes more concerned. The banging is now accompanied by muffled yelps. BOGDAN looks around to see if anyone is watching him. As he puts his hand on the doorknob, he is interrupted by FLOYD.*

FLOYD
(wheeling in a gurney) Bogdan! How are you, my friend?

BOGDAN
(realizing it is FLOYD) Futui.

> *BOGDAN quickly removes his hand from the doorknob and continues mopping.*

FLOYD
Always cleaning up the mess we make. Better you than me, eh, Buddy?

BOGDAN
(pointing to the door of the broom closet, speaking in broken English) Door.

FLOYD   Yes, Bogdan. That *is* a door.

BOGDAN   Locked.

FLOYD   Come again?

BOGDAN   Cineva este in spatele usii. Te rog ajuta!

FLOYD   Your language is very pretty.

BOGDAN   *(mimics muffled noises)*

FLOYD   Your English is improving. Excuse me while I dispose if this corpse.

> *Exit FLOYD.*

> *A note slips out from under the door. BOGDAN reads it, consulting his dictionary. After figuring out what the note says, he gasps, wide-eyed. More urgently, he tries again to open the door, trying various keys, none of which work.*

BOGDAN   *(muttering anxiously)* Dear God. Oh, dear God. *(calling to anyone in particular)* Ajutati-ma!

> Enter FLOYD.

FLOYD   *(hurrying to BOGDAN'S aid)* Take it easy.

BOGDAN   Doctor.

FLOYD   The doctor is with a patient.

BOGDAN   Listen.

FLOYD   No time. You see, I have a very important job.

BOGDAN   Janitor.

FLOYD   Yes, Bogdan. You *are* a janitor.

BOGDAN   Doctor!

FLOYD   *Nurse.* Can you say *nurse?*

BOGDAN   Woman.

FLOYD   That stings, Bogdan. It really does.

>*Muffled yelps are heard from behind the closet door.*

BOGDAN   You hear?

FLOYD   *(not seeming to hear the yelps)* Yes, Bogdan. I'm here. But I have to go.

BOGDAN   Listen inside.

FLOYD   Yes, Bogdan. If we listen inside, we can hear a still, small voice, telling us to do the right thing.

BOGDAN   Nu! Doctor!

FLOYD   *(gesturing towards himself)* Nurse. *(pointing to examination room)* The doctor is with a patient.

BOGDAN   Listen...

FLOYD   Can't Bogdan. I want to listen to you, but I can't.

BOGDAN   But...

FLOYD   I'm getting ointment for Dr. Mendax. It's one of the many important things that I do.

Exit FLOYD.

BOGDAN   Este un idiot.

                              BOGDAN scrambles to find a key that fits in the door.

BOGDAN   *(to the yelper)* Is okay! I hear! *(anxiously muttering)* Help, God. Help.

SCENE THREE

Examination room.

MENDAX   It's normal to be in shock. Denial. Don't get too comfy. Once the numbness wears off and the depression kicks in, you'll most likely feel like offing yourself before your six months are up.

SHYLIE   I don't understand.

MENDAX   Let me explain. You have a plantar wart, which means the wart is growing inward instead of outward. It will begin in your foot and gradually extend throughout your entire body until it reaches your brain. At this point, it will wrap itself like fingers, around your cerebrum and squeeze.

> *BOGDAN, still trying different keys to open the closet door, overhears and grimaces.*

MENDAX   Yes, it will squeeze your brain like an orange.

> *BOGDAN eavesdrops with his ear against the door.*

MENDAX   It will squeeze all the ideas out of your brain until you die. Unfortunately, there is nothing we can do to stop it.

SHYLIE   This is all so unbelievable.

> BOGDAN attempts to take a chart from outside the door of the examination room. FLOYD catches BOGDAN as he returns to the examination room with the ointment. FLOYD slaps BOGDAN'S hand. BOGDAN continues mopping, muttering. FLOYD enters the examination room.

FLOYD   Ointment.

SHYLIE   Do you think I should get a second opinion?

MENDAX   Why?

SHYLIE   We are talking about my life.

MENDAX   If you can't trust your life with a doctor...

FLOYD   Dr. Mendax?

MENDAX   Yes, what?

FLOYD   The drug rep is here to see you.

SHYLIE   What about me?

MENDAX   What *about* you?

SHYLIE   I am going to die.

MENDAX   Not for six months. You'll be here when I return.

SHYLIE   But...

                                    *Exit MENDAX. SHYLIE is left alone
                                    with FLOYD.*

FLOYD   I'm fond of women, in case you were wondering.

SHYLIE   What?

FLOYD   Want to get some sushi?

SHYLIE   Stop flirting.

FLOYD   Why?

SHYLIE   I'm going to die.

FLOYD   What's wrong with friendly, heterosexual banter?

SHYLIE   Should I quit my job?

FLOYD   I make an above average income.

SHYLIE   I've never been to Europe.

FLOYD   Let's go then. You and me.

SHYLIE   I should call home.

FLOYD   Home?

SHYLIE   None of this would be happening if I still lived at home.
                Nothing bad ever happens in Mosquito's Elbow.

FLOYD   What in frigging heck is Mosquito's Elbow?

SHYLIE   My home. The smallest town in Northern Ontario.

FLOYD   Really.

SHYLIE   Only twenty-six people live there. The McMeghans next door. The O'Shannons across the street. The Raisin. *(explaining)* The old man who runs the mercantile. There's Reverend Finnigan. Dr. Seamus. The blacksmith. The tinker.

FLOYD   What's a tinker?

SHYLIE   What's a tinker? Really, Floyd. You certainly are sheltered.

FLOYD   Seriously. What's a tinker?

SHYLIE   The tinker fancied me.

FLOYD   He what?

SHYLIE   So did Reverend Finnigan. The reverend was much more reasonably aged than the tinker. And rather fetching. But I was much too worldly to be a minister's wife.

FLOYD   Worldly?

SHYLIE   I completed a university degree through correspondence. That didn't go over too well in the town.

FLOYD   Want some pills?

SHYLIE   I was banned from the quilting guild. My parents still won't talk to me.

FLOYD   *(doesn't care)* Shame.

SHYLIE   What I miss the most is the little diner on the waterfront. Miss Agnes made trout so fresh, it would flake right off your fork. And you had your choice of potatoes prepared in five different ways. Potatoes from the O'Shannon's garden.

FLOYD   I have access to lots of pills.

SHYLIE   Toronto isn't safe. Not like home.

FLOYD   You're in a hospital. You're safe.

SHYLIE   I shouldn't have moved here.

FLOYD   Why *did* you?

SHYLIE   I wanted to see the world I read about in books. I thought I had time.

FLOYD   Let's hop on a plane to Cuba.

SHYLIE   I can't.

FLOYD   Why not?

SHYLIE   You can get hepatitis from the ice cubes.

FLOYD   Let's go back to your place then.

SHYLIE   I'm scared of my apartment.

FLOYD   Wha?

SHYLIE   I can hear the subway grumbling beneath me. It's disturbing.

FLOYD   Disturbed. Hmm.

SHYLIE   What I need is...

FLOYD   Me.

SHYLIE   You?

FLOYD   Both of us win.

SHYLIE   How?

FLOYD   Women are fond of meaningful relationships.

SHYLIE   Yes.

FLOYD   I want to copulate.

SHYLIE   That's profane.

FLOYD   Do you want to go running back to the fetching, Reverend Finnigan?

SHYLIE   Leave the reverend out of this. That's personal.

FLOYD   Have you ever kissed a guy even?

SHYLIE   Shut it.

FLOYD   How could you? Living in Mosquito's Elbow where cousins breed?

SHYLIE   *(gasps in disgust)*

                                        Enter   MENDAX,   wearing   a Caribbean shirt.

MENDAX   Just met with the drug rep. *(handing SHYLIE some pills)* Take these.

SHYLIE   What are these pills for?

MENDAX   Depression.

SHYLIE   I'm not depressed.

MENDAX   You're depressing the hell out of me.

SHYLIE   What?

MENDAX   You are going to die. Dying is depressing.

SHYLIE   But...

MENDAX   The drug is called Propaxoft. I prescribe it to all my patients regardless of the problem. The effects will kick in immediately if you remove your clothing.

SHYLIE	Remove my clothing?
FLOYD	You heard the doctor.
SHYLIE	I don't need...
MENDAX	I'll tell you what you need.
SHYLIE	This sort of thing would never happen in Mosquito's Elbow.
MENDAX	Mosquito's Elbow? Susan, she's speaking in riddles.
FLOYD	It's her kinky hometown in Northern Ontario. Don't ask about the tinker.
SHYLIE	Dr. Seamus was discreet. He would never violate me in this manner.
MENDAX	I don't give a flying frig how a red-necked quack runs his practice in some backwoods hamlet. You are in the city. I am a highly strung, city doctor with many ailing patients. The highlight of my day does not involve birthing a litter of piglets.
SHYLIE	Dr. Seamus would never...
MENDAX	Do I look like Dr. Seamus? Does Dr. Seamus have my throbbing temples? My palpitating heart? Beads of sweat dripping from his brow? I have many patients. Real patients. All of whom have six months to live. Do you know how much stress...
FLOYD	Doctor, your face is turning an unusual shade of red.

MENDAX	Ms. McBean, if you do not co-operate, you will add me to the ever-increasing tally of suicidal doctors. Is that what you are tying to do? Are you trying to kill me?
SHYLIE	No. I just need...
FLOYD	Me.
SHYLIE	No.
MENDAX	I'll write another prescription. You'll need lots of these.
FLOYD	But Dr. Mendax...
MENDAX	*(to FLOYD, aside)* We won't get paid unless I write a prescription or perform a procedure. Now, unless you want me to slowly remove her foot with an emery board...
FLOYD	*(turning to SHYLIE)* Listen to the doctor. He is all-knowing. Somewhat like a god.
MENDAX	*(to SHYLIE)* Why aren't you naked?
SHYLIE	I...
MENDAX	Shylie, the anti-depressant will have a delayed effect if you don't de-clothe yourself entirely.
SHYLIE	But...
MENDAX	Fine. *(handing SHYLIE a hospital gown)* If you must, find a change room and put on this hospital gown.

SHYLIE   To take a pill?

FLOYD   You won't be naked, but your hindquarters will be
                embarrassingly exposed.

MENDAX   Susan.

FLOYD   Hmm?

MENDAX   Show some decorum.

                                    Exit SHYLIE with hospital gown.
                                    Before she leaves, she looks
                                    uncertainly at MENDAX and
                                    FLOYD.

FLOYD   Propaxoft?

MENDAX   The drug rep says it contains agents of all the other
                anti-depressants combined.

FLOYD   Question.

MENDAX   Hmmm.

FLOYD   On the off chance that Shylie doesn't need anti-
                depressants...

MENDAX   Susan...

FLOYD   I'm not saying you're wrong. I'm just saying if there
                isn't an imbalance in her brain, won't the anti-
                depressants create an imbalance that will result in

suicidal tendencies?

MENDAX   You think you know more than I?

FLOYD   Absolutely not. You are like the Pope of Medicine. But in my RN program...

MENDAX   Do you have any more questions or are you hoping that your stupidity will cause a rise in my stress barometer, which will eventually cause me to implode?

FLOYD   No more questions.

MENDAX   Good.

FLOYD   One more question.

MENDAX   Grunt.

FLOYD   Does Shylie really have to remove her clothing for the drug to take immediate effect?

                                    MENXAX gives FLOYD an icy stare.

FLOYD   Stupid question.

MENDAX   She'll be more likely to believe me if she's naked.

FLOYD   Come again?

MENDAX   Makes her vulnerable.

FLOYD   Sure.

MENDAX   And we want her to believe me.

FLOYD   Of course we do. You're a doctor. You know what's best. Like this drug, for instance.

MENDAX   Propaxoft is truly a remarkable drug. If I prescribe it to one hundred and six patients, I will be entitled to an all-inclusive vacation in Barbados.

FLOYD   Barbados?

MENDAX   Barbados is just what I need to keep me from removing my own face with a scalpel.

FLOYD   And being the highly trained professional you are, that will in no way sway your judgment.

MENDAX   Do you have any idea what the suicide rate is among doctors?

FLOYD   I'm not really a numbers guy.

MENDAX   It's better that way. The rate is so staggeringly high, it might give you a nosebleed.

FLOYD   No doubt.

MENDAX   How convenient that I can write prescriptions for myself.

FLOYD   Come again?

MENDAX   For each prescription, I receive a hefty wad from OHIP.

For each prescription, I can etch another stick on my tally for a much needed vacation by a sea of turquoise. With each prescription, my tumultuous life becomes that much more bearable.

FLOYD   Propaxoft can do all that?

MENDAX   Is your head made of cheese? I save the good stuff for myself.

FLOYD   What's the good stuff?

MENDAX   If you ever become a doctor, you will be privy to such information.

FLOYD   A doctor!

MENDAX   But we both know that will never happen.

FLOYD   Oh.

MENDAX   This, I can tell you. The drugs I prescribe myself have the power to unravel the tension in my brain like a loose thread on a cheap sweater. They can erase data from my cerebrum like the delete button on my McIntosh. The stimuli in these pills are potent enough to make pleasant thoughts spontaneously pop into my mind like happy kernels of hot corn. My brain becomes numb with glee. Much needed glee.

FLOYD   Dr. Mendax...

MENDAX   Everyday I tell people they are going to die.

FLOYD   Like a god.

MENDAX   This kind of power is exhausting.

FLOYD   All that wrath to pour. All those Philistines to smite.

MENDAX   Do you think I *enjoy* ending lives?

FLOYD   I...I don't know.

MENDAX   Would *you?*

FLOYD   Sort of. I mean, people believe your words like the gospel. They just...die.

MENDAX   Power can be crippling. It can make your levels a little off.

FLOYD   Well sure. Altering a person's will to live...

MENDAX   I speak it and it happens.

FLOYD   I wish I could control minds.

MENDAX   Is that what you think I do?

FLOYD   Um...I don't know.

MENDAX   You think I do this on purpose?

FLOYD   I...

MENDAX   Do you think I'm controlling your mind right now?

FLOYD   Of course not. That would be absurd.

MENDAX   What kind of a sick shit do you think I am?

FLOYD   You're not a...

MENDAX   This is what doctors do, Susan.

FLOYD   Of course. You would never...

MENDAX   I'm just doing my job.

SCENE FOUR

> BOGDAN is mopping. Once again, he hears knocking coming from behind the door of the janitor's closet. Just as BOGDAN is about to open the door, SHYLIE arrives, looking for a change room in which to change into a hospital gown. SHYLIE notices BOGDAN and shyly approaches him.

SHYLIE   Do you know where I might find a change room?

BOGDAN   Nu! Leave! Go! Flee! Do the vamoose!

SHYLIE   *(suddenly afraid of BOGDAN'S accent)* I...I didn't realize you...excuse me.

BOGDAN   Shylie.

SHYLIE   How do you know my name?

BOGDAN   Danger.

SHYLIE   *How do you know my name?*

BOGDAN   Mendax. He is a...he is a...

SHYLIE   You're freaking me out.

BOGDAN   Shylie.

SHYLIE   Stop calling me that.

BOGDAN   Listen.

SHYLIE   I need to change. *(gesturing to janitor's closet)* Is this the change room?

BOGDAN   Closet.

SHYLIE   Close it?

BOGDAN   Closet.

SHYLIE   It's closed.

BOGDAN   Nu, Shylie. Closet.

SHYLIE   I don't understand.

BOGDAN   Understand.

SHYLIE   I don't understand what you're saying to me. Please stop.

BOGDAN   Bad things, Shylie.

SHYLIE   You're frightening me.

BOGDAN   Don't die.

SHYLIE   What?

BOGDAN   You. Don't do the death. Not time.

SHYLIE   Nobody has time to die, Scary Man. I don't want to talk
                about it. Just let me...*(tries door to closet)*

BOGDAN   Exit! Door out!

                                    SHYLIE turns the doorknob on the
                                    closet and muffled cries are heard
                                    from within. The noise frightens
                                    her and she runs away.

SCENE FIVE

> *MENDAX is writing in SHYLIE'S chart. BOGDAN watches MENDAX. MENDAX ignores him.*

BOGDAN   I know.

MENDAX   You know nothing.

> *BOGDAN grabs chart from MENDAX.*

BOGDAN   You are wrong.

MENDAX   *(grabbing chart back)* Am I? Seems a janitor knows more about medicine than a fully qualified practitioner. Curious.

> *BOGDAN grabs chart from MENDAX.*

BOGDAN   Nu!

MENDAX   *(grabbing chart)* Know your place!

BOGDAN   You have no...voices in your head!

MENDAX   Voices in my head.

BOGDAN   Constiinta.

MENDAX   What?

BOGDAN   *(reading from dictionary)* Con...science.

MENDAX   I'm ignoring you.

BOGDAN   Mendax, girl may die.

MENDAX   Of course. She'll die when I tell her to.

BOGDAN   Not God.

MENDAX   I have figured out the way things work.

BOGDAN   But...

MENDAX   You wouldn't want me to go to the janitor's union and tell them they have a Romanian miscreant at large.

BOGDAN   Is wrong.

MENDAX   It's not wrong. It's just the way things work.

SCENE SIX

Examination room. FLOYD is alone.

CASSETTE   You are a strong, virile man.

FLOYD   *(with eyes closed)* Strong, virile man.

CASSETTE   You are in control.

FLOYD   In control.

CASSETTE   Your muscles are hard and unforgiving, like avalanching boulders.

FLOYD   Muscles.

CASSETTE   You contain all the correct members of the male anatomy.

FLOYD   Strong, virile man.

CASSETTE   You have the shoulders of an albatross, chiseled biceps and the butt of a statue.

FLOYD   David.

CASSETTE   You have a surplus of sperm which swims through your body like pink, spawning salmon.

FLOYD   Fish.

CASSETTE   You have raw, animal energy and are propelled by brute strength and testosterone.

FLOYD   Strong, virile man.

CASSETTE   There is nothing wrong with being a...

                                        The cassette jams. FLOYD sits bolt upright with wide eyes. SHYLIE enters. Both are startled. FLOYD, as a reflex, pulls out a large, dripping syringe.

SHYLIE   Good God!

FLOYD   Yeesh!

SHYLIE   What's with the dripping syringe?

FLOYD   Isn't it large?

SHYLIE   What?

FLOYD   Do you know what's in this needle?

SHYLIE   No.

FLOYD   I do.

SHYLIE   I put on this hospital gown as I was told.

FLOYD   I have access to all the needles in this building.

SHYLIE   So you've said.

FLOYD   Does that impress you?

SHYLIE   *(calling)* Dr. Mendax?

FLOYD   Why are you so obsessed with Dr. Mendax?

SHYLIE   Why are *you* so obsessed with Dr. Mendax?

FLOYD   Mendax is likened unto the vengeful God of the Old Testament. But that's beside the point.

SHYLIE   Oh my god!

FLOYD   He won't be back for several minutes.

SHYLIE   Mendax or God?

FLOYD   Same thing.

SHYLIE   But Reverend Finnigan used to say...

FLOYD   Slut.

SHYLIE   What?

FLOYD   Going around de-frocking Finnigans.

SHYLIE   I didn't...Give me my clothes.

FLOYD   That's not bureaucratically possible.

SHYLIE   Why?

FLOYD   Hospital policy. You wouldn't understand.

SHYLIE   I have to get out of here!

FLOYD   Why are you in such a hurry? We've barely gotten to know each other. How can we possibly begin our lives together...

SHYLIE   My life is not beginning. It's ending.

FLOYD   We can buy a bungalow on the West End. I can paint it orange.

SHYLIE   Orange?

FLOYD   We'll sit on the porch as we watch our children at play.

SHYLIE   When did we have children?

FLOYD   We'll have four children. Two girls and three boys, all of whom resemble me. You can see them frolicking on our chemically treated front lawn.

SHYLIE   We'll have time to do all this in six months?

FLOYD   Am I making you hot?

SHYLIE   I am going to die! Besides, you are the last person...

FLOYD   *(poising syringe)* Relax.

SHYLIE You're scaring me. Everything in this building scares me. The stark walls. The squeaking gurneys. The stagnant air. The beeping. That vile, hospital odour that smells like what happens when urine, death and chicken broth breed!

FLOYD *(approaching with dripping syringe)* I'll give you a little something to help you relax.

SHYLIE I don't want to relax! Where is Dr. Mendax?

FLOYD *(administering injection into SHYLIE'S arm)* Hospital business.

> *SHYLIE instantly becomes unconscious.*

FLOYD *(caressing SHYLIE'S unconscious face)* It's all hospital business.

SCENE SEVEN

> The broom closet door. The muffled yelps are heard. MENDAX walks past, not hearing the yelps. BOGDAN, looks at MENDAX in disbelief. MENDAX downs a bottle of pills. The yelps get louder. BOGDAN struggles with the doorknob. His keys don't fit the door.

BOGDAN   Constiinta!

> No response from MENDAX.

BOGDAN   You deaf?

> Still, no response.

BOGDAN   Voice inside!

> Still, no response. As MENDAX walks away, keys fall from his cloak. BOGDAN tries to swipe the keys, but MENDAX gets to them first. Both have their hands on the keys. They stare into one another's eyes. A pause as they stare each other down.

MENDAX   Keys, Bogdan.

BOGDAN   *(pointing to door)* Inside.

MENDAX   You're hearing things. Shall I call the Psych Ward?

BOGDAN   Nu.

MENDAX   Fine. Then give...me...the...*(grabs keys away)* keys.

                              They stare at each other as MENDAX backs away.

SCENE EIGHT

> *The examination room. The room is set up as though a romantic dinner is in progress. (mellow music, candles, table) FLOYD is wearing a bow tie over his scrubs. SHYLIE, is unconscious, slumped limply in a chair at the table. BOGDAN is in the hallway, mopping. He overhears everything.*

FLOYD   The cabernet this evening is rather fruity. Wouldn't you say so, my darling Shylie?

> *FLOYD makes SHYLIE move like a puppet.*

PUPPET   You have exquisite taste, my sinewy specimen of manhood.

FLOYD   Only the best for my dainty flower. Shall I top up your goblet?

PUPPET   Oh! I musn't, lest I lose my virginal inhibitions.

FLOYD   Tut, tut, my sweet. Mine are motives of purity.

PUPPET   I feel so safe.

FLOYD   Would you care for some pheasant?

PUPPET   You eat it, my steaming vial of testosterone.

FLOYD   *(taking pheasant from SHYLIE'S plate)* You are so demure.

PUPPET   I am in the company of a chiseled, mythological god.

FLOYD   Oh, Shylie, my wilting daisy.

PUPPET   I worship you.

FLOYD   Shall I kiss you on the lips?

PUPPET   Will it be a sin?

FLOYD   Of which the blood of Christ will not redeem.

PUPPET   Then yes. I would like that very much.

                                            FLOYD snuffs out the candles, clumsily clears the table off with one fell swoop of his arm and lunges awkwardly at SHYLIE'S unconscious body. He kisses her. BOGDAN bangs on the door from the hallway.

BOGDAN   *(banging on door from hallway)* Awaken! Trezeste-te inainte ca ceva groaznic sa se intmple! Esti in pericol! Asculta-ma! Dear God, Shylie! Dear God!

                                            SHYLIE wakes up to find FLOYD kissing her passionately. FLOYD continues to mimic her with his eyes shut.

FLOYD   Oh, Floyd! My id is screaming! Do you hear my screaming id?

SHYLIE   Unhand me!

FLOYD   It's not what it looks like!

SHYLIE   Get away from me, you freak show!

FLOYD   I can explain.

SHYLIE   I'm leaving.

FLOYD   You can't.

SHYLIE   Clearly, I'm not safe here.

FLOYD   No place is safer than a hospital.

SHYLIE   You did profane things to me in my sleep!

FLOYD   Define profane.

SHYLIE   You are a warped man and there is something very crooked about this whole hospital.

FLOYD   I have your clothes.

SHYLIE   Keep them. I'm leaving.

Enter MENDAX, wearing a

hospital mask.

MENDAX   You are not going anywhere, Ms. McBean.

FLOYD   See?

MENDAX   The results of your tests have arrived from the lab.

SHYLIE   Tests?

MENDAX   *(putting a mask on Shylie)* The tests indicate that Shylie has a highly contagious, airborne foot virus. She must never leave.

SHYLIE   What?

MENDAX   There is a deadly, communicable disease, contaminating the hospital's air supply. No one is to enter or leave the building. Especially you, Ms. McBean.

FLOYD   Can I have a mask too?

MENDAX   No.

SHYLIE   When will I be allowed to go home?

MENDAX   Shylie, you are chronically ill. Your condition will slowly worsen until the life is snuffed out of you like the luminaries in a drafty, Catholic church.

SHYLIE   I want to leave.

MENDAX   And endanger the community with your toxic feet? How vile.

FLOYD   At least we can be together.

MENDAX   Both of you sicken me.

                              BOGDAN overhears and shakes his head in disgust. He mops.

BOGDAN   Why, Bogdan, why?

SHYLIE   I can never leave?

MENDAX   You make it sound foreboding.

SHYLIE   I don't want to die here.

                              BOGDAN takes the chart from the door without anyone seeing.

BOGDAN   *(writing in chart)* Because I should.

MENDAX   The choice is not yours to make.

SCENE NINE

> *MENDAX comes out of the examination room, partially stoned. He catches BOGDAN writing in the chart.*

MENDAX   Miscreant!

BOGDAN   *(replacing chart)* Bogdan fix.

MENDAX   Tampering with a patient's medical records!

BOGDAN   *(pointing to chart)* Truth! Read!

MENDAX   You are a janitor.

BOGDAN   You have no voices!

MENDAX   I'm ignoring you.

BOGDAN   You fear Bogdan.

MENDAX   What's that? Fear? Have you given any thought to what will happen if I report you to the janitor's union?

BOGDAN   I know.

MENDAX   Do you understand the ramifications of tampering with a patient's chart?

BOGDAN   Da.

MENDAX   Do you?

BOGDAN   Stop tormenting of the Bogdan! He will not break!

MENDAX   Oh, I can break you.

> BOGDAN *raises his hand to strike*
> *MENDAX, but stops himself.*

MENDAX   Do it.

BOGDAN   Nu.

MENDAX   Hit me.

BOGDAN   Should not.

MENDAX   You won't strike a doctor, but your scruples are few enough to scribble unintelligible, Romanian jargon in the chart of a patient.

BOGDAN   Da.

MENDAX   Why?

BOGDAN   Because I should!

> MENDAX *staggers, as though*
> *stoned.*

MENDAX   You're making no sense.

BOGDAN   Constiinta!

MENDAX   *(holding head)* Mop, damn you!

                              MENDAX doubles over. BOGDAN gestures as though trying to decide whether or not he should help MENDAX. FLOYD bursts out of the examination room and into the hallway, in search of MENDAX.

FLOYD   Dr. Mendax...*(noticing BOGDAN)* Bogdan! How's my favourite Romanian?

BOGDAN   *(gesturing to MENDAX)* In need!

FLOYD   What are you in need of, Confrere?

BOGDAN   *(shaking MENDAX, who has passed out)* Drugs.

FLOYD   Of which you have not been prescribed?

BOGDAN   Taci si asculta la mine.

FLOYD   Did I mention today what a superlative job you are doing? Seriously, Bogdan. I could lick the floor.

BOGDAN   As vrea sa te vad pe tine facand asta.

FLOYD   I have no idea what you just said, but I like the way you said it.

BOGDAN   Sunt singurul care stie ce vorbeste din aceasta cladire.

FLOYD   If you say so.

Muffled yelps and knocking come from inside the janitor's broom closet. MENDAX does not hear because he is still passed out. FLOYD simply does not hear.

FLOYD   *(in reference to the closet)* I didn't hear that.

BOGDAN   *(gesturing to the closet)* Again! Listen!

FLOYD   I am always listening, Bogdan. I am your friend.

BOGDAN   *(gesturing to the closet)* Listen inside!

FLOYD   Yes, Bogdan. As I've mentioned on a number of occasions, we must always listen to that ambiguous, little voice inside us, telling us to do the right thing.

BOGDAN   Closet!

FLOYD   Close it?

BOGDAN   Closet!

FLOYD   Close what?

BOGDAN   *(pounding palm against the door)* Closet!

FLOYD   The door is already closed, Bogdan. Please focus.

MENDAX groans.

FLOYD   Is something wrong with Dr. Mendax?

BOGDAN   Much things wrong.

FLOYD   It's not drugs.

                              MENDAX moans.

BOGDAN   I know.

                              MENDAX moans.

FLOYD   Dr. Mendax! Wake up! Bogdan knows!

                              BOGDAN resumes mopping.

FLOYD   Bogdan! Wait! You can't just know things and then
               walk away! That's elusive!

                              *BOGDAN gives FLOYD an eerie
                              stare.*

FLOYD   Why are you looking at me that way? It's making me
               feel uncomfortable. Stop it, please.

                              BOGDAN maintains his stare.

FLOYD   Please stop.

MENDAX   *(moaning himself awake)* Susan?

FLOYD   Yes, Dr. Mendax?

MENDAX   Who are you talking to?

> *There is a brief pause as FLOYD casts one, last look at BOGDAN, who remains staring at FLOYD.*

FLOYD   No one of any importance.

SCENE TEN

SHYLIE is alone in the examination room. She talks to herself, removing her hospital mask.

SHYLIE   I'm at their mercy. My body doesn't even belong to me anymore. It's all so peculiar. A year ago the biggest problem I had was deciding whether I was wearing enough layers of flannel while paddling my canoe. I swatted some blackflies. The crickets kept me up sometimes. And on occasion, Miss Agnes ran out of trout. That little town seemed so reclusive. Mosquito's Elbow was the only place where I felt truly free. I saw moose. And mist swirling atop the lake at six in the morning when the air is crisp. And God help me, I love the smell of bug repellent. Why did I ever leave?

Enter BOGDAN, mopping the examination room. SHYLIE gasps, curling herself up in a ball, hiding her feet. There is a brief pause a As they look at one another.

BOGDAN   Bogdan Cosminescu.

SHYLIE   What?

BOGDAN   My name.

SHYLIE   Oh.

Brief, awkward pause.

BOGDAN   *(gesturing to SHYLIE'S feet)* May I?

SHYLIE   You shouldn't be in here. I have this foot virus.

> *BOGDAN closes the door.*

SHYLIE   Why did you do that?

BOGDAN   Foot please.

SHYLIE   *(turning away)* Absolutely not.

BOGDAN   Shylie...

SHYLIE   *(still turned away)* My feet are personal. I was saving them for someone special.

> *BOGDAN washes his hands with his back facing SHYLIE.*

BOGDAN   Bogdan here to help.

SHYLIE   *(scared but curious)* Your accent...is it...

BOGDAN   Hmm?

SHYLIE   Nothing.

BOGDAN   Hmm.

> *SHYLIE cannot help but look at BOGDAN while his back is turned. She quickly turns her back to him*

when BOGDAN turns to face her.

BOGDAN   *(taking SHYLIE'S foot and looking at it)* If you listen, I help.

SHYLIE   Don't touch me! Good God! Rape! Help! An immigrant has my foot!

BOGDAN   I make you a favour.

SHYLIE   Why?

BOGDAN   Feeling the right thing to do. You know. Heart voices. Constiinta.

SHYLIE   *(confused for a moment, then gets it)* You mean conscience?

BOGDAN   You having?

SHYLIE   Everyone has a conscience.

BOGDAN   Nu.

As BOGDAN investigates SHYLIE'S foot, SHYLIE yelps out in pain.

BOGDAN   Shylie hurt?

SHYLIE   I'm okay, I think.

BOGDAN and SHYLIE look at each other.

SHYLIE   I mean, I think I'm okay.

                                    A beat.

SHYLIE   *(quickly, before she changes her mind)* Are there
                mountains?

BOGDAN   Pardon?

SHYLIE   You're from Romania, right?

BOGDAN   Da.

SHYLIE   I read in a book...I mean, I completed a university
                degree through correspondence...European Studies. I
                was just wondering...

BOGDAN   *(smiling)* Da.

SHYLIE   Da? There's mountains. I've never seen one before.
                Could you tell me about the...*(remembering that she is
                shy)*...You're nice. Why.

                                BOGDAN looks sad.

SHYLIE   *(noticing she said something wrong, changing subject)*
                The mountains must have been so beautiful. Why on
                earth would you want to leave Romania?

                                    *BOGDAN shows SHYLIE a
                                    photograph.*

SHYLIE   *(looking at photo)* She's pretty. Is this your daughter?

BOGDAN   *(blinking back tears)* Daughter. Named Catina.

SHYLIE   Is she in Romania?

BOGDAN   *(nodding)* Is hard.

SHYLIE   Bogdan...

BOGDAN   In the ground.

SHYLIE   She's...dead?

BOGDAN   Sick. Lungs. Could not save...

SHYLIE   What?

BOGDAN   You having Catina's face.

SHYLIE   I look like her.

BOGDAN   Don't die.

SHYLIE   I hardly have a choice in the matter.

BOGDAN   Don't letting them have your *mind!*

> *Enter MENDAX, who is just a little bit more stoned than he previously was. SHYLIE is startled and hides her feet. BOGDAN shakes his head in disgust.*

MENDAX   Susan! Janitor handling foot!

SHYLIE   Dr. Mendax...

MENDAX   *(to BOGDAN)* Ruffian! First the chart and now the foot!

SHYLIE   But...

MENDAX   *(to BOGDAN)* You are unqualified!

BOGDAN   The girl...

MENDAX   The girl has nothing to do with this, you knave. This is between the two of us!

BOGDAN   She...

MENDAX   She has a highly contagious, airborne foot virus. One that I, myself, diagnosed not moments ago. Were you aware of that, Knave?

BOGDAN   I should...

MENDAX   And here you are, ungloved, handling the infected appendage, while millions of lethal spores are wafting from that wart.

BOGDAN   I should...

                                    MENDAX attempts to detain BOGDAN. BOGDAN is much bigger and stronger than MENDAX.

MENDAX   Susan! I have detained the Romanian! I need backup!

BOGDAN   Nimeni in aceasta cladire nu are constiinta!

                                    FLOYD rushes in.

FLOYD   Doctor?

MENDAX   The immigrant must be detained!

FLOYD   *(helping MENDAX detain BOGDAN)* I'm on it!

SHYLIE   Bogdan!

BOGDAN   Run!

SHYLIE   But...

BOGDAN   Go!

SHYLIE   What about my clothes?

BOGDAN   Forget!

SHYLIE   About my clothes?

BOGDAN   Iesi afara pana mai poti!

                              SHYLIE is torn. After a brief pause,
                              SHYLIE runs out of the
                              examination room.

MENDAX   What the...

FLOYD   She's escaped!

MENDAX   Get her!

FLOYD   Seriously?

MENDAX   Go!

FLOYD   Going!

> *FLOYD runs out of the examination room. BOGDAN and MENDAX are left alone in the room. MENDAX has run out of steam and must stop his struggle with BOGDAN in order to catch his breath.*

MENDAX   I won't let you get the better of me.

BOGDAN   I know.

MENDAX   Stop saying you know. What could you possibly know?

BOGDAN   Bogdan know Mendax.

MENDAX   How could you? Are you saying you're able to creep into my ear and bounce around in my brain tissue like the walls of an asylum? You have no idea why I...

> *MENDAX has a dizzy spell.*

BOGDAN   Will die.

MENDAX   Shylie? I gave her six months to live. Of course she'll...

BOGDAN   You.

MENDAX   What?

BOGDAN   Not Shylie.

MENDAX   You make no sense.

BOGDAN   You die.

MENDAX   I'm ignoring you.

BOGDAN   Mistake.

MENDAX   Doctors don't make mistakes.

BOGDAN   Stop this.

MENDAX   And give up everything I...*(dizzy spell)* And give up the...And give up...give up...

BOGDAN   Mendax...

MENDAX   The agony!

MENDAX collapses, but remains conscious. BOGDAN attempts to help MENDAX.

BOGDAN   Mendax!

MENDAX   Don't touch me!

BOGDAN   Incerc sa ajut.

MENDAX   Give me the pills, you lousy foreigner! I know who you
                are and I know you know what I mean and I know you
                know how to...

BOGDAN   Help.

MENDAX   I don't want the help of an immigrant!

BOGDAN   Bogdan is a...

> *MENDAX clumsily rises to his feet,
> grabs BOGDAN'S mop, staggers
> awkwardly and hits BOGDAN with
> the mop, knocking BOGDAN
> down.*

MENDAX   Mop!

SCENE ELEVEN

The hallway. SHYLIE frantically runs on stage, stops, wide-eyed, facing the audience for a brief moment and then runs frantically offstage in a different direction. FLOYD runs on stage, flailing and whimpering like a ninny. After running a few frantic laps around the stage, he runs, flailing and whimpering offstage in a different direction. MENDAX staggers onstage, even more stoned than he was previously. He doubles over in agony. He stumbles on the stage, but picks himself back up, pulls a pill bottle out of his pocket, downs the entire bottle and staggers offstage in a different direction. BOGDAN, with his cleaning gear, makes his way into the audience's space. During the rest of the scene, BOGDAN remains in the audience's space, cleaning. While the scene's action takes place, BOGDAN mops up and down the rows of seats in the audience. He cleans various objects. BOGDAN occasionally notices the happenings on the stage and occasionally mutters and shakes his head in disgust. He continues throughout the scene, until the stage directions indicate otherwise. This scene is reminiscent of a Feydeau play. As SHYLIE, MENDAX and FLOYD run on and off the stage, they do so in very opposite directions, narrowly missing each other. It is imperative that the action in this scene moves at an extremely fast pace.

SHYLIE runs onstage.

SHYLIE   My clothes!

SHYLIE runs offstage.

FLOYD runs onstage.

FLOYD   My importance!

FLOYD runs offstage.

MENDAX staggers onstage.

MENDAX   Pills!

MENDAX staggers offstage.

SHYLIE runs onstage.

SHYLIE   *(scared of FLOYD)* Floyd!

SHYLIE runs offstage.

FLOYD runs onstage.

FLOYD   Shylie!

FLOYD runs offstage.

MENDAX staggers onstage.

MENDAX   Susan!

MENDAX staggers offstage.

FLOYD runs onstage.

FLOYD   Dr. Mendax?

FLOYD runs offstage.

SHYLIE runs onstage.

SHYLIE   *(scared of MENDAX)* Dr. Mendax!

SHYLIE runs offstage.

MENDAX staggers onstage.

MENDAX   Ms. McBean!

MENDAX staggers offstage.

SHYLIE runs onstage.

SHYLIE   Bogdan!

> *SHYLIE runs offstage.*

> *FLOYD runs onstage.*

FLOYD   Floyd!

> *FLOYD runs offstage.*

> *SHYLIE runs onstage.*

SHYLIE   I have to get out of here!

> *SHYLIE runs offstage.*

> *MENDAX staggers onstage.*

MENDAX   Need pills!

> *MENDAX staggers offstage.*

> *FLOYD runs onstage.*

FLOYD   I need you, Shylie!

> *FLOYD runs offstage.*

> *SHYLIE runs onstage.*

SHYLIE   Floyd! I need my clothes back!

> *SHYLIE runs offstage.*

> *MENDAX staggers onstage.*

MENDAX   Susan! You have access to all the pills in the building!

MENDAX staggers offstage.

SHYLIE runs onstage.

SHYLIE   Come on, Floyd! I can't go anywhere without my clothes!

SHYLIE runs offstage.

FLOYD runs onstage.

FLOYD   I'm a man!

FLOYD runs offstage.

MENDAX staggers onstage.

MENDAX   Where is Shylie? I'm losing my patience!

MENDAX staggers offstage.

FLOYD runs onstage.

FLOYD   Is there a God?

FLOYD runs offstage.

MENDAX staggers onstage.

MENDAX   Did somebody call me?

MENDAX staggers offstage.

FLOYD runs onstage.

FLOYD   My ears hear you, Dr. Mendax!

FLOYD runs offstage.

SHYLIE runs onstage.

SHYLIE   Out! Out! Out! Out! Out! Out! Out! Out!

SHYLIE runs offstage.

FLOYD runs onstage.

FLOYD   Shylie? Is that you?

FLOYD runs offstage.

MENDAX   *(from offstage)* Susan! Need!

FLOYD   Coming, Dr. Mendax!

FLOYD runs offstage.

SHYLIE runs onstage.

SHYLIE   How do I get out of here? *(notices door of the janitor's closet)* Door!

SHYLIE opens the door. It is not an exit. What she sees makes her scream. SHYLIE slams the door shut and runs offstage, screaming.

FLOYD runs onstage.

FLOYD   Shylie?

FLOYD runs offstage.

MENDAX staggers onstage.

MENDAX   Susan?

MENDAX staggers offstage.

SHYLIE runs onstage.

SHYLIE   Bogdan!

BOGDAN'S ears perk up as he is in the audience, doing his schtick. He turns towards the stage and looks at SHYLIE from the audience's space.

BOGDAN   *(in audience)* Shylie?

FLOYD runs onstage at the same time that MENDAX staggers onto the stage. SHYLIE is cornered.

SHYLIE   I...it...door...I...

MENDAX   Make some sense, Girl.

SHYLIE   I thought that door was an exit. It isn't.

MENDAX   She's crazy. Tie her up, Susan.

FLOYD   What did you see, Shylie?

SHYLIE   I saw...

MENDAX   Brooms. It's a janitor's broom closet. She saw brooms.

FLOYD   How would you know?

SHYLIE   A man.

FLOYD   What?

SHYLIE   There was a man in the broom closet.

MENDAX   No.

SHYLIE   He was wearing a white doctor's coat, a stethoscope around his neck and a nametag that said...

MENDAX   Shut up!

SHYLIE   Dr. Mendax. His nametag said Dr. Mendax.

FLOYD   It said...what?

SHYLIE   That's what I saw.

FLOYD	But Dr. Mendax is Dr. Mendax. Aren't you, Dr. Mendax?
MENDAX	Of course I'm Dr. Mendax.
FLOYD	But...
MENDAX	Who are you going to believe, Susan? A pig-tailed hick from Mosquito's Elbow or a high profile physician?

> *FLOYD looks back and forth from SHYLIE to MENDAX. FLOYD opens the door to the janitor's broom closet. There are muffled yelps for help. The audience does not see what FLOYD sees. After briefly examining the sight he sees in the closet, FLOYD slams the door shut.*

FLOYD	*(matter-of-factly)* There's a doctor in there.
MENDAX	I had nothing to do with it.
FLOYD	How long has he been in there, do you suppose?
MENDAX	Nearly a year.
FLOYD	What?
MENDAX	I mean, I have no idea.
FLOYD	You just said...

MENDAX   I'm stoned.

SHYLIE   He survived in there for nearly a year?

FLOYD   *(peeking behind the door and closing it again)* Looks like he's been drinking the hospital's supply of Ensure.

MENDAX   That's smart.

> *BOGDAN raises a finger to comment on FLOYD'S closing of the door, then decides it's no use.*

SHYLIE   I thought I heard strange noises coming from behind that door.

FLOYD   Why did I not hear all those yelps? I mean, if the guy's been in there for nearly a year...

> *More muffled yelps are heard from behind the door of the broom closet. SHYLIE, FLOYD and MENDAX are so caught up in their conversation, nobody pays the muffled yelps any mind, nor do they seem to notice the pounding on the door.*

SHYLIE   But who is the doctor in the broom closet?

MENDAX   Mendax.

FLOYD   What?

MENDAX   I mean, I'm stoned.

SHYLIE   If Dr. Mendax is in the broom closet, then who is...

                                MENDAX collapses.

FLOYD   Dr. Mendax! Dear God! We need a doctor!

                        *BOGDAN hurries from the
                        audience's space and makes his
                        way to the stage.*

BOGDAN   Is here.

FLOYD   Bogdan, find a doctor!

BOGDAN   Is!

FLOYD   Is what?

BOGDAN   Doctor.

FLOYD   Who?

BOGDAN   Bogdan.

FLOYD   Listen, Bogdan, if this is some sort of Romanian
              humour, it doesn't translate well.

BOGDAN   *(pushing FLOYD out of the way)* Move.

SHYLIE   What is Bogdan doing?

BOGDAN   Doctor.

FLOYD   The doctor is in the close it. Hey, I just got that.

BOGDAN   Janitor.

FLOYD   We are aware that you are a...

BOGDAN   Not Bogdan! *(pointing at MENDAX)* Him!

FLOYD   Dr. Mendax?

BOGDAN   Mendax is janitor. Bogdan is doctor.

FLOYD   What?

SHYLIE   Dear God!

FLOYD   A doctor? You?

BOGDAN   From Romania.

SHYLIE   Bogdan is a doctor from Romania.

FLOYD   I don't believe this.

SHYLIE   Why is that so difficult to believe?

BOGDAN   Doctor me. No games with lives. No games with head. No God games. Come to help.

FLOYD   What is he talking about?

SHYLIE   Bogdan is a doctor. He wants to help.

FLOYD   But he's mopping the floor.

BOGDAN   *(lovingly to SHYLIE)* One life I save. No?

> *SHYLIE is moved. BOGDAN intrigues her.*
>
> *MENDAX moans on the floor, as he awakens from his unconscious state.*

FLOYD   He is risen!

MENDAX   Susan?

FLOYD   Your humble servant has come to perfume your feet and anoint your forehead with fragrant oils.

MENDAX   *(moans)*

FLOYD   *(to MENDAX)* You're not a janitor. Tell me you're not a janitor.

MENDAX   He should have died.

FLOYD   Who?

MENDAX   Why won't he just die? The pounding. The yelping. The relentless voice inside...

FLOYD   Inside the closet?

>> *Muffled yelps from behind the door.*

MENDAX   Nobody listen!

BOGDAN   Doctor.

>> *Muffled yelps.*

MENDAX   *(to door)* Shut up, or I'll give you six months to live! *(to others)* That goes for all of you!

SHYLIE   How did you get away with this?

MENDAX   Why aren't you naked?

SHYLIE   You've stolen the identity of a physician, locked the real doctor in a broom closet for nearly a year and assumed his podiatry practice for the entire time. How is it that you weren't caught?

MENDAX   Things around here have a way of slipping through the cracks.

FLOYD   *(re-locking closet door and discreetly hiding key on his person)* Bureaucratic nightmare. Only this morning, I filled out some paperwork to take a mental health leave, and somehow, all the documentation mysteriously...

MENDAX   Shut up, Susan.

SHYLIE   Are you some kind of sociopath?

MENDAX   I'll be making the diagnoses, thank you very much.

SHYLIE   You fraud! This is identity theft!

FLOYD   I won't accept this.

SHYLIE   How on earth did you get away with...

MENDAX   Oh, come off it! Like I'm the first! This sort of thing happens all the time! Some forged signatures, false references, blackmail. Now. Who wants ice-cream?

SHYLIE   Have you no conscience?

MENDAX   Hey, you're the one with the problem. Not me. After all, I DID get away with this for a year. Now if one of these three Susans would just make this room stop spinning...

SHYLIE   I don't believe this. You told me I was going to die.

MENDAX   You are...Someday.

FLOYD   (as BOGDAN is trying to open the locked closet door) All this is Bogdan's fault. He knew the real doctor was in the broom closet. Why didn't you say something, Bogdan?

BOGDAN   Tried.

FLOYD   Why didn't you let the man out of the closet yourself?

BOGDAN   Locked.

FLOYD   Answer me! Why didn't you do anything? Why didn't you help? Why?

BOGDAN   *(angry and frustrated)* Am incercat sa va spun despre omul din dulap dar nimeni nu m-a ascultat! Si am incercat sa deschid usa si sa-l eliberez de mai multe ori insa tot timpul am fost oprit! Nu mi se permite sa fac nimic! Nu mi se permite sa spun nimic! Tot ce sunt lasat sa fac este sa spal podeaua, sa spal podeaua, sa spal podeaua, sa spal podeaua! Aveti idée cat de frustrant este? Doamn Dumnezeule! Tara asta este condusa de maimute! Futui! Duca-se la dracu!

FLOYD   Such pretty noises.

                  BOGDAN points to the door and then waves it away as to say, "Never mind." Nobody is paying him any mind.

MENDAX   *(in agony)* Oh God!

FLOYD   He's talking to himself! Somebody do something!

BOGDAN   I help.

MENDAX   Stay away from me, you Communist beast!

SHYLIE   He's only trying to...

MENDAX   *(cringing)* Help!

BOGDAN   Dying.

MENDAX   *(hisses like a cat as BOGDAN backs away)* I don't want his help!

FLOYD   Please!

MENDAX   I will not allow that miscreant to put his hands upon me!

BOGDAN   Listen.

SHYLIE   Yes, listen.

FLOYD   Please, listen. If you listen carefully, there's a little Romanian inside all of us. Telling us to do the right thing.

MENDAX   There is no little Romanian inside me!

SHYLIE   Why?

MENDAX   What?

SHYLIE   Why did you do all this?

MENDAX   *(choking and sputtering)* Because I can.

> *A weird, blue light momentarily illuminates the stage as a choir of angels sing one, long note of a requiem. MENDAX'S eyes bug open during this ridiculously brief moment. The light and angel note abruptly stop and MENDAX is dead. BOGDAN checks MENDAX'S*

> *pulse and nods to confirm the death of MENDAX.*
>
> *FLOYD is hysterical.*

FLOYD   Our lord is dead! My god! My god!

BOGDAN   El nu mai avea nici o constiinta. Era mort deja.

FLOYD   *(to corpse)* Arise! Resurrect! *(shaking corpse)* Perform a miracle on yourself, damn you!

BOGDAN   *(pulling SHYLIE'S clothes out the garbage)* Is dead.

SHYLIE   *(taking her clothes from BOGDAN)* He always was.

FLOYD   What am I supposed to do now? I have no purpose. I have no God. No direction. I...Shylie?

SHYLIE   You're looking at me.

FLOYD   That life I dreamed up for the two of us.

SHYLIE   Absolutely not.

> *SHYLIE leaves briefly to change into her clothes.*

FLOYD   *(calling after SHYLIE)* As it seems, you're not going to die in six months.

BOGDAN   Floyd. Get life.

FLOYD   *(in awe)* That is so proverbial! Somewhat like a prophet! St. Bogdan of Assisi! Do you mind if I call you that?

                      BOGDAN rolls his eyes and shakes his head in disgust. SHYLIE returns, fully dressed in her own clothes.

SHYLIE   *(to BOGDAN, a little uncertain)* Um...hey.

BOGDAN   *(trying the word out in his mouth)*...Hey...*(looks for word in dictionary)*

SHYLIE   Esti prietenul meu. Multumesc pentru tot ce ai facut pentru mine.

                      BOGDAN looks surprised and confused.

SHYLIE   European Studies.

BOGDAN   Cu placere, prietene.

                      SHYLIE is momentarily confused.

SHYLIE   It was just a correspondence course.

                      SHYLIE begins to leave. She stops herself. She briefly re-approaches BOGDAN and looks at him inquisitively for a moment.

SHYLIE   Where's a good place to stay in Bucharest?

BOGDAN   You going? To my home?

SHYLIE   I thought I'd try...*(passing her phone number)* Here. In
                case you can recommend some hotels, touristy things.
                Stuff like that. I trust your judgment.

BOGDAN   Smart girl. Just like...*(stops, saddened)*

                                    *After briefly looking at BOGDAN,
                                    SHYLIE scurries away.*

BOGDAN   *(emotionally to SHYLIE)* Good Bye, Catina.

SHYLIE   *(stops)* Excuse me?

BOGDAN   *(bowing head)* Shylie.

SHYLIE   *(pulling BOGDAN'S chin up)* I'll be okay.

BOGDAN   *(turning up SHYLIE'S collar)* Keep warm.

                                    BOGDAN watches SHYLIE leave.

FLOYD   The giver of life! That's who you are, Bogdan! Not the
                elusive janitor we all thought you to be! Isn't that right,
                Bogdan?...Bogdan?

                                    *The stage blacks out and FLOYD
                                    fades into the darkness until he
                                    disappears. BOGDAN is left alone
                                    on the stage, isolated by a
                                    spotlight. BOGDAN mops the
                                    floor, but stops himself when he
                                    notices MENDAX, lying dead on*

the stage, wearing a white, doctor's coat. BOGDAN approaches the corpse, removes the coat and puts it on himself. BOGDAN admires the coat he is wearing. But then BOGDAN notices his mopping equipment. He shakes his head, re-approaches his mop and bucket, and continues mopping. BOGDAN hears the muffled yelps. He takes a set of keys from MENDAX's pocket and unlocks the door which opens with a conspicuous creak. The audience cannot see who is in there. But now "he" is free to go if he wishes. BOGDAN shakes his head as he looks at MENDAX on the floor and resumes mopping.

BOGDAN   Someone must clean up this mess.

Finis.

www.ingramcontent.com/pod-product-compliance
Lightning Source LLC
Chambersburg PA
CBHW032109170626
46808CB00008B/2987

* 9 7 8 1 7 7 7 2 2 0 3 1 0 *